WRATH IN THE MIDDLE

Bishop Billie Jackson

Published by BOTR Press, LLC

Copyright 2020   Bishop Billie Jackson
Published by BOTR Press, LLC
Poplarville, MS
www.BOTRPress.com

Cover photographs by Oziel Gomez, Marina Kazmirova, Laura Margarita Cedeno Peralta, Dr.Josiah Sarpong and Suzana Sousa on unsplash.com
Graphics by Mary Beth Magee

*"Be ye angry, and sin not:
let not the sun go down upon your
wrath:
Neither give place to the devil."*

Ephesians 4: 26-27

This book is dedicated to three women who God used in helping me finish this work

My wife, Prophetess Carolyn Jackson
First Lady Anna Turner
Minister Mary Beth Magee

WRATH
IN THE
MIDDLE

Bishop Billie Jackson

Introduction

"Be ye angry, and sin not; let not
the sun go down on your wrath."
Ephesians 4:26

In my many years as a pastor, I've seen a lot of marriages. I've seen the problems that can come up in a marriage. One of the biggest problems I've seen, again and again, is the Wrath in the Middle.

The wrath is a creature of the devil who goes to bed with a saved couple, if they lay down to sleep without forgiving any hurts of the day. He gets right up in the middle between them. He can talk and oh, he does talk. His job is to take a little hurt, a little slight and make it hurt more and grow bigger until that couple just can't stand to stay together anymore.

As believers, we serve a powerful God. He can defeat Wrath every time. All we have to do is call on Him and claim His power.

As you read this book, think about how Wrath works, not just in marriages but in life. He comes to destroy. God sent His Son to heal. Who will you let in the middle of your life?

1

Bishop Billie Jackson

Chapter One

"Blessed is every one that feareth
the LORD; that walketh in his
ways. For thou shalt eat the
labour of thine hands: happy
shalt thou be, and it shall be well
with thee. Thy wife shall be as a
fruitful vine by the sides of thine
house: thy children like olive
plants round about thy table.
Behold, that thus shall the man
be blessed that feareth the
LORD." Psalm 128:1-4

Rene Miller snuggled a little closer to her husband as they crossed the parking lot of the multiplex. The initial crowd which had poured out of the theater doors along with them thinned as the couple moved from one pool of light to another across the warm asphalt.

"You know, honey, I really enjoyed this time together, just the two of us, you and me. No kids, no family or friends, not even our church family around. I mean, I love them all, but we earned us a little 'just us' time," Arthur said. He stopped for a moment and gazed into her eyes, smiling at the woman he loved. A stray lock of hair blew across her face and he brushed it away with his free hand before sweeping her brow with a whisper of a kiss.

"Yes, sweetie, this is nice," Rene responded as they resumed their journey toward the car. "I really enjoyed our quiet dinner, and then that movie! Wow, it was so funny, I nearly fell off my chair laughing. Good thing you had an arm around me to keep me from falling." She laughed and leaned her head against his shoulder as they walked.

"You can always count on me to keep you from falling, baby," he said. "But oh, man, did you see how that man took that car..."

"Yeah," she interrupted. "Oh, yeah!" Her laugh speeded up to a giggling fit.

"...and when they took that man out of that..." He laughed with her.

"Yeah, yeah, that car! That was so funny!!!" Rene laughed so hard she could barely catch her breath.

"Yes, it was." Arthur stopped once again. He slid his arm out of Rene's and took both her delicate hands in his larger ones. He lost himself in her dark eyes again. He stopped laughing and his voice deepened to a husky bass as he continued. "Rene, it is so good to see you smiling and having fun for a change. You spend so much of yourself on others that I worry about you taking care of yourself."

She looked up into her husband's eyes and saw the genuine love shining there. "Well, I could say the same about you. I'm glad to see you relaxed and not so uptight!" She smiled at him and they laughed together.

"Come on, let's go home," she said. "I hope that son and daughter of ours have not turned our house inside out while we were gone."

Arthur held Rene's hand as she slid into the car. He wrapped a kiss in her palm before closing the door for her. When he entered the driver's seat, she leaned over to kiss his cheek before she fastened her seatbelt. The warmth of mutual love and respect filled the car. Neither of them noticed the shadowy figure watching from the edge of the building as they pulled out of the parking lot and headed home.

Bishop Billie Jackson

Chapter Two

"…what doth the LORD thy God
require of thee, but to fear the
LORD thy God, to walk in all his
ways, and to love him, and to
serve the LORD thy God with all
thy heart and with all thy soul,
To keep the commandments of
the LORD, and his statutes, which
I command thee this day for thy
good?" Deuteronomy 10:12-13

Every window in the house glowed as
Arthur pulled into their driveway.

"What in the world?" Arthur's expression
shifted from "man in love" to "father in
frustration" in the blink of an eye.

As they exited the car, they were assailed
with the pounding bass of loud music and
explosions coming from the house. Arthur
motioned Rene behind him as they headed for
the door. Whatever the source of the commotion
inside, he would try to shield her.

He eased open the front door and peeked
inside. He spotted his son Malcolm sprawled
across the sofa, head weighed down by a virtual
reality gaming headset. The teenager could have
been a giant insect for all of his goggle-eyed
appearance. The evidence of a meal based on
snack foods littered the couch and floor.
Another explosion sounded from the flat-screen

television on the wall and Malcolm let out a whoop, barely audible over the music.

The couple stepped into the room, pushing against the wall of noise. Neither of them noticed the shadow which followed them into the house.

Across the living room, Malcolm's younger sister Marie sat cross-legged in Arthur's recliner. Her head bent over her phone, fingers flying across the keyboard, she didn't notice her parents enter the house. The screen of the device she had propped on the end table at her left elbow danced with the movement of the characters on the program she watched over the top of her phone and a canned laugh track poured out of the speaker.

Arthur took in a deep breath and prepared to yell to the kids, but he felt Rene's gentle touch on his arm.

"Not tonight, honey. Let's not ruin our evening." Her soft voice in his ear barely overcame the noise of the devices. "Please, not tonight."

He nodded his agreement. She was right. No sense ruining the pleasant evening they had shared by getting angry. He thanked God silently for the wisdom of his beautiful wife.

"Okay, honey," he replied. Then he raised his voice to a loud, but warm tone. "Hey, kids, we're home!"

The shadowy figure frowned and glared at Arthur. His squinted gaze focused like a laser on the man's heart.

Malcolm responded to Arthur's greeting by sliding the goggles from his head and turning toward his parents with a smile. Marie gave no indication she had heard Arthur's words.

Rene stepped closed to Arthur, watching for his reaction and praying he would handle the situation well.

"Hey, Mom, Dad. When did you two get back?" Malcolm turned back to the game screen as a vehicle sped across it, tires squealing at a painful pitch.

"Hey, son," Rene offered, but Malcolm didn't seem to hear her.

"Son, could you turn that music down, please?" Arthur paused as Malcolm reached for the portable sound system on the coffee table. He tried to keep his voice level when he continued, but he could hear himself get louder and feel the agitation build. "Do you really need all these lights on? Do you think we own stock in the power company or something?"

Malcolm's smile faded as he felt the sting of his father's words.

"Oh, I was trying to drown out Marie's TV. I can't stand that stupid sitcom she's watching. Plus, I was listening to that new group 'Ozell Atkins & C-Nation.' Their new album is featured tonight. Man, Dad, you got to hear them. They are…"

"Mommy, Daddy! You're home! When did you get home?" Marie squealed as she bounded out of the overstuffed chair in her excitement. She ran to her mother's arms.

"Hi, baby. We just walked in." Rene hugged her daughter close. "Have you finished your chores and taken your bath yet? Or have you been on that phone ever since we left?"

"She's been texting and talking and watching TV the whole time you been gone. She ain't done nothing else but sit over there in Daddy's chair like she owned it." Malcolm was quick to testify against his little sister.

The shade in the corner came to attention.

"Like you've done anything but play your stupid game and listen to your loud music," Marie shouted in response. One corner of the shade's mouth lifted in pleasure.

Arthur felt his fists clench as tensions escalated in the living room.

"Stop it, both of you!" He looked around the living room. "Malcolm, before you say another word, you need to close down that game and pick up all this snack trash. Take it out of here. It doesn't look like either of you've done anything toward your chores since we've been gone either. And Marie, don't yell at your brother."

In an effort to control his rising temper, Arthur walked away from the two kids and headed into the kitchen.

"Kids, you better get going and finish your chores. Then get ready for bed." Rene gave her instructions in a quiet tone. "I want this room presentable when I get back in here."

The children exchanged a glance as Rene left the room. Each of them considered the other one to be the one at fault. They began picking up the room under an uneasy truce. The shadowy figure in the corner smiled at their discomfort.

Rene went into the kitchen to talk to Arthur. She found him seated at the kitchen table, head bowed, and hands clasped. His lips moved in a silent prayer. She waited until he finished praying before joining him at the table.

"Honey, the kids are working on their chores. Would you c'mon and go to our room with me? I want to talk to you about something."

"Sure, baby." He looked into her face. "Did I overreact to the kids? I tried to keep calm, but they can be so irresponsible…"

She patted his hand. "No, you didn't overreact. They were trying to push your buttons, turning on each other like that. C'mon, honey."

They rose from the table and held hands as they headed to the hallway toward their bedroom. Before they reached the bedroom door, the doorbell rang.

"Ma, it's Ms. Helen," called Malcolm.

"What in the world does she want at this hour?" asked Arthur.

"I don't know, but I'll find out. I'll be back in a minute or two." She kissed Arthur before she turned back toward the living room.

She entered the living room but didn't notice the shadowy figure in the corner who listened with close attention. His eyes glittered with interest.

"Hey, lady, what are you doing out so late?" Rene asked her friend.

"Well, girl, you didn't answer your telephone and I thought you and Arthur should be off your date by now. I just took a chance to come over. I mean, it's not like ya'll hang out a lot. I mean, don't get me wrong; I know you're both busy. With him in Ministry and you working, and y'all kids and stuff…"

"Girl! Get on track. What did you want?" Rene's mind was on getting back to some time with her husband. She didn't want their pleasant, relaxing evening to end yet. Her voice sharpened in irritation with Helen Bradford's interruption and rambling. The shade smiled.

12

"Oh...well...look, I'll get to the point. I need you to help me with the bake sale and toy drive tomorrow, and--"

"Oh, no. You wait a minute, wait...a... minute! We already told the church and everyone else, *including you*, that Arthur and I would not be available this weekend. We are going to Florida for the weekend," Rene couldn't believe Helen would have the nerve to ask her for help at this late date. She shook her head. "Uh-uh, no, not this weekend, no way."

Disappointment and disbelief washed over Helen's face. She couldn't believe her dependable friend would turn her down this way.

"Oh, c'mon, Rene! Please," she begged. "You know I can't do this by myself. I need you to help me. You're the only one I can count on. *Ple-e-easezzz.*" She turned baby doll eyes on Rene, then crossed her fingers behind her back for luck.

The shadowy figure smiled again, a satisfied smile. He could always count on weak, suggestible Helen to be a helpful tool in his plans.

Rene stared at her friend, shocked at Helen's behavior. She dropped her voice until it was barely above a whisper but carried the weight of a sledgehammer. "Helen, now you know how long I've been waiting for this getaway. I will not give it up. I can't. No, not this weekend. I just can't."

"But it's for the church, Rene. You know I wouldn't ask you if it was just some old personal favor." Her voice struck Rene as sounding like a whining child, begging for a treat. "You are the only one who can make those good old homemade cheesecakes. Everyone will be looking for them, you know they will. We won't make any money for the church without them."

Helen's flattery chipped away at Rene's resolve. She gave a tiny smile and nodded her head yes to the compliment while her mind raced to figure a way to help Helen and still spend time with her husband.

"Oh, ALRIGHT, alright. Stop already. I'll help you...*oof.*" Rene almost fell as Helen barreled into her with a tight hug. "But I can only stay for a short time. I've got to get ready so Arthur and I can leave for Florida in the morning."

The shade in the corner smiled even wider. The plan was in motion.

"Ok, girl. That's fine. I just need you to help me set up for the sale, prepare and you know, do what you do best." Helen wisely hid her triumph under cover of gratitude.

Rene sighed, tired and frustrated at her friend's expectations. "It's already late and I'm tired. Now I have to bake some cheesecakes. Fine. How many do you need?"

"Oh, not many. Just a few. Ten or twenty will be fine. That's all." Helen's off-hand delivery didn't cushion the blow to Rene's feelings.

"Ten or twenty? Girl, have you lost your mind?! I'll be up baking all night. What time does this thing start?" Her sharp tone cut at Helen.

"Umm, set-up is at 6 a.m.," she replied, as she drew back, almost afraid to speak in the face of her friend's response.

"6 a.m.? It's already 10:30!!" Rene couldn't hold back her anger any longer. She started to push Helen toward the door. "Look, you got to go. I've got to go to the store for supplies, bake your precious cheesecakes, pack for the trip…just get out of my way. I've got too much to do and no time to do it in. I'll see you in the morning at the church."

Helen stumbled out the door with Rene's hand in her back. She cast a confused look back at her friend before Rene closed the door. What had happened to her sweet, easygoing friend? She shook her head and trotted to her car. She felt lucky to still have her head on her shoulders.

Rene leaned against the front door, overwhelmed by Helen's requests. Malcolm and

Marie stared at her, surprised by her outburst. When she saw their expressions, she hovered between defensiveness and anger.

"Have you finished your work yet? Get those chores done and get to bed!" she snapped.

She looked toward the hallway. *How am I going to explain this to Arthur?* she thought. *He won't understand why I'm not in there snuggling with him. Oh, never mind!* She grabbed her purse and headed out to the all-night supermarket.

The shade in the corner nodded in satisfaction.

Chapter Three

"Live joyfully with the wife whom thou lovest all the days of the life of thy vanity, which he hath given thee under the sun, all the days of thy vanity: for that is thy portion in this life, and in thy labour which thou takest under the sun. Whatsoever thy hand findeth to do, do it with thy might; for there is no work, nor device, nor knowledge, nor wisdom, in the grave, whither thou goest" Ecclesiastes 9:9-10

The clock on the stove read 3:25 when Rene took the last of the cheesecakes out and turned the oven off. She threw the potholder onto the counter and headed to the bathroom to change into her nightclothes before going into the bedroom. The rest of the clean up could wait for help from the kids.

In the faint moonlight coming through the window, she could make out Arthur's outline on the bed. Quietly as she could, she slipped out of her slippers and robe. She sat on the edge of the bed and moved to snuggle with her husband.

Arthur woke up and turned away from her. "So, you decided to let Helen talk you into helping her instead of coming in here with me?" The coldness in his voice shocked Rene as much as the sight of his back turned toward her.

17

"Honey, you know how it is. When it comes to the church, it's hard for me to say 'no' and that Helen doesn't make it easy for me to tell her 'no,' either." She used her best soothing tone of voice and reached out her hand to touch his shoulder.

Arthur shrugged off her hand. "Yeah, I hear you. It's hard for you to tell her no, but it's not hard for you to put me off." His voice dripped sarcasm. She recoiled in hurt from his angry words.

He turned over to look at her. "We have been planning this trip for months. I told the church we would not be available. I even cancelled the basketball game with the fellas so I could spend time with you. Doesn't that mean anything to you?"

Guilt washed over Rene as his words sank in. "You know it does, honey. We can still leave in the morning. I'm just going to take the pies over to Helen and help her set up. Then I'll come straight home and we can leave. I shouldn't be gone more than an hour. We'll still be on the road on time."

The shadow in the corner watched in amusement as she tried to placate her husband.

"Rene, it is after 3:30 in the morning and you are just now coming to bed. I heard her tell you the bake sale and toy drive will start at setting up at 6 a.m. That means you have to leave here no later than 5:30 to help her with set up. And you haven't packed for the trip yet."

"I'll finish packing as soon as I get home. It will…"

"You know when you get there you ALWAYS start talking and never come back when you're supposed to. This is the kind of stuff I tell you that bothers me. You can always find time to do everything for everyone else and I'm always second on your list. That just isn't right!"

Rene sat up on the edge of the bed. Her feelings shifted from apologetic to downright angry. "What do you mean 'this is what you tell me,' huh? I could see you with something to complain about if I was lollygagging around, but I'm busy doing things for the church where you are one of the ministers! I would think YOU would be happy I'm doing this, being a good preacher's wife."

She took a deep breath and tried to calm down. "I mean, c'mon Arthur. Let's go to sleep so I can get up in two hours and we can make plans to leave at 9:30 instead of 6:30." She tried to think sweet thoughts. "It's only a three-hour difference."

Arthur exploded from the bed. His voice rose with each word. "You just don't get it! It's not the three-hour difference, it's the fact that **you chose** to push our time back. You **chose** to stay up baking pies tonight instead of us

19

spending the rest of the evening together. Now you've **chose** to go off to a bake sale and you don't think anything is wrong with it because it's for the church!" He took two steps closer to the edge of the bed, staring down at her.

"You don't get a lot of things, Rene. Like earlier tonight when we came home. Malcolm had that music blasting; every light was on in the house and all you could do was tell ME not to get mad! Me!! And I'm the daddy! I'm the one taking care of things around here, not him. But you told me not to get mad. Once again, you put me second in my own house." He turned away from her and crawled back in the bed. He pulled the covers up to his chin as tight as he could. "Enough, Rene. It's enough."

The shade in the corner swelled with joy. Perfect!

Rene paused at his words. Who did he think he was talking to that way?

"Now wait a minute! You are not the only one taking care of things around here. And I tried to calm you down because your first reaction is always to fuss. That's all you do! You find fault and you fuss about everything! And we get tired of it." Her voice climbed in pitch. "I don't know what makes you think I put you second when every time I look up you are gone. You're gone to the church, gone to the gym working out, you're off playing basketball, and doing *I don't know what* because you don't tell me! Don't even go there with me! And yes,

I am doing stuff for the church. I'm trying to *support* your church. If you can't understand that, then that's just too bad! Deal with it!"

Wrath felt happiness throughout. His plan was working beautifully.

He sat up in the bed. His voice struck her like ice. "Oh, I'll deal with it alright! I'll tell you what. Cancel the reservation for the hotel for this weekend. I'm not going nowhere with you. Why should I spend time with someone I can't trust to keep her word?"

"Can't trust?! I'll tell you what. You can just cancel the reservation yourself if you want it cancelled. I'm not doing nothing. I can't believe you, Arthur! You would cancel our trip just because I'm going to a bake sale for an hour?! That is really sad. How can you be so selfish? And call yourself a *man of God*? Hah!" Rene was determined to give as good back as she got. What had gotten into him tonight?

The shadowy figure moved closer to hear every delightful word. He didn't want to miss a single syllable.

"Selfish, am I? Well, I am a man of God, whether you believe it or not. Don't talk to me anymore, Rene, please! Because you are only making me mad. I wanted to spend time with my wife tonight and you are telling me I'm selfish!! I plan a vacation with my wife and I'm selfish? And you accuse me of *calling* myself a man of God. Woman, please! That's just fine, you go to your bake sale. I'll spend the weekend by myself in Florida." He plopped down on his pillow.

"Oh, no, you won't," she yelled.

"Watch me! I'm not cancelling nothing. I'm keeping the reservation and going by myself! Now scoot over to your side of this bed and leave me alone." He pushed her further away, then turned his back to her.

"Don't you push me, 'cuz I don't want to touch you anyway! It's 4 o'clock in the morning and I really don't want to talk to you anymore. I can't believe you." She punched her pillow. Her words were filled with sarcasm and bile. *"Can't trust me, hah!* Just stay on your side of the bed and don't you touch me. *I'm going to Florida by myself! Uh!* I wish he would. Heavenly Father, I pray that you will forgive my husband for treating me the way he does. Please strengthen him in his mind, Lord, and show him the right path. Please bless my family and church family. Please bless our bake sale and toy drive, Lord, and show the scoffers how hard we work on Your behalf. And, Lord, please give me strength to deal with my husband. Amen." That would show him!

Arthur wouldn't be outdone. "Lord, thank you for blessing me to be able to take a trip to Florida by myself. I thank you for allowing me to have a wife that puts the church affairs over her husband's needs. Bless my family, and

Lord, thank you for allowing me to have a safe and fun trip without my wife."

He heard her derisive snort before he fell into a troubled sleep.

The shadowy figure, Wrath, left the corner and glided to the bed. He slithered between the backs of the angry couple and situated himself snugly in the middle. No longer a gray shadow, he now showed red from head to toe.

"He don't love you. Look at him over there asleep." Wrath whispered in Rene's ear as she slept. She writhed in agitation at his words. "You should put a pillow over his head. Leave him. Stop caring for him. He always fussing anyway. You can take care of yourself and the children by yourself." She continued to twist in her uneasy sleep.

Wrath turned to Arthur. "She don't understand you. Other women would be glad to have you. Find you some new stuff! She thinks you are weak. Show her you aren't. Go on that trip by yourself and have fun. When you get back, don't even talk to her for a month. Show her who is really the head of this house." Arthur huffed in his sleep.

The red figure spent the remaining few hours of the night between the two of them, a crimson barrier to reconciliation. The smile on his face took on a malicious tilt as the

23

atmosphere in the bedroom grew colder and colder.

Arthur struggled with unsettling dreams before he gave up and rose at 5 a.m. By 6:30, he was on the road, on the way to his solo trip to Florida.

Chapter Four

"A soft answer turneth away
wrath: but grievous words stir up
anger. The tongue of the wise
useth knowledge aright: but the
mouth of fools poureth out
foolishness. The eyes of the
LORD are in every place,
beholding the evil and the good.
A wholesome tongue is a tree of
life: but perverseness therein is a
breach in the spirit." Proverbs
15:1-4

Rene arrived at the church at 5:30 a.m.
When she brought in the eighteen cheesecakes
and handed them over to Helen's care, she
didn't notice the specter who had hitched a ride
in her car.

"I'll be able to stay and help you after all,"
she told Helen. "Arthur and I changed our plans.
You know how devoted we both are to the
wellbeing of this church." She ignored the ache
filling her heart as her friend smiled.

"See, I told you I could count on you, if I
couldn't count on nobody else," Helen said.
"Lord knows, the church has been generous in
their donations of baked goods, but they forget I
need somebody to help me run the show."

Rene helped Helen arrange the wide
assortment of donated goods in attractive

displays throughout the fellowship hall. She had to admit the sight of all those beautiful cakes, pies and cookies filled her soul with joy. If everything sold, the church's building fund would reap great benefits today.

Two other women arrived at last to help sell the goodies and process the toys brought in by donors. With only four workers there was hardly a moment for the ladies to rest. When Jenna Carson's husband stopped by at 11 with a tray of sandwiches, he expressed his surprise at the scarcity of helpers.

"When will Pastor Arthur come over?" he asked. "You ladies will need some strong backs to help with those boxes of toys. I surely can't move them all by myself."

Rene hemmed and hawed for a moment. "Arthur is working on a special project," she finally stammered. "He won't be coming in to help today. Maybe you could round up a few other fellows to move the boxes."

Helen froze with a sandwich halfway to her mouth. "I thought you said he was so committed to the church's welfare. What could be more important than helping us get the children's toy ministry set up?"

Wrath smiled from his vantage point near the coffeemaker. How would Rene handle this little minefield? Each lie strengthened his control over her.

"Well, I don't know all the details. The situation came up sort of sudden-like. I just know he'll handle it the best he can." Rene could feel the heat of embarrassment creeping up her neck.

"I'll keep his project in my prayers," said Roland Carson. "I'm sure it's just as important as what we're doing here."

"Thank you, Brother Carson," Rene said. "I'm sure he'll appreciate your prayers."

By the time Rene got home that evening, she was physically exhausted and emotionally drained. In the privacy of her bedroom, she kicked the shoes off her swollen feet and vented to her reflection in the mirror.

"How many times they going to ask where Arthur is? I don't want to be telling lies to my church family. How dare that man leave me in this position! How can I ever forgive this behavior of his?"

She wished she could attribute the ashen tone of her skin to working so hard today, but she knew there was more than old-fashioned tired involved. A hovering cloud of guilt reminded her of her sharp answers to her husband last night.

"Will he come home again?" she wondered. "Do I even want him to come home again? This has turned into such a mess. All I wanted to do was help the church fundraiser. What's wrong with that?"

The Rene in the mirror didn't offer any answers, but Wrath stood in the corner and focused his attention on the distraught woman.

"Nothin', that's what wrong with it," she told herself. "Nothin' but his mixed-up head. Huh!"

Wrath smiled.

"Hey, Ma, what's for dinner?" Malcolm's voice boomed down the hall.

At least that part of her world was still normal.

Chapter Five

"Put on therefore, as the elect of
God, holy and beloved, bowels
of mercies, kindness, humbleness
of mind, meekness,
longsuffering; Forbearing one
another, and forgiving one
another, if any man have a
quarrel against any: even as
Christ forgave you, so also do ye.
And above all these things put on
charity, which is the bond of
perfectness. And let the peace of
God rule in your hearts, to the
which also ye are called in one
body; and be ye thankful. Let the
word of Christ dwell in you
richly in all wisdom; teaching
and admonishing one another in
psalms and hymns and spiritual
songs, singing with grace in your
hearts to the Lord." Colossians
3:12-16

Three weeks later, the situation had not
improved. Rene slept in the bedroom alone.
Arthur slept on the couch. Rather than the hot
boil of the initial conflict, the anger between the
two had settled to a constant simmer. They
weren't talking to each other or displaying any
positive attitude. Neither made a move toward
reconciliation. Wrath floated from one to the
other, pricking their spirits with his lies.

Rene's mother arrived at 8 a.m. and knocked on the door. When Rene opened it, the two women embraced. Over her daughter's shoulder, Mary could see Arthur on the couch. He was wrapped in a blanket and squeezing a pillow as if it was a lifeline.

"Hey, baby. How are you today?" she asked Rene.

"Hi, Mama. I'm fine. Come on in."

"Are you sure?" Mary asked as she entered the home. She pointed toward Arthur. "What's going on, Rene? For the last three weeks, every time I come by here, Arthur has been asleep on the couch. I could understand him falling asleep on the couch one or two nights, but, baby! C'mon. Something is not right."

"Mama, everything is just fine. He fell asleep watching a movie." Mary parroted with her "...*fell asleep watching a movie.*"

"Honey, you can't hide anything from me. I was married to your father for 46 years, and there were many nights he *fell asleep on the couch watching TV.* Hah! You can't fool me, baby. But I will tell you, three weeks is too long for your husband to be falling asleep on the couch. You know what the Word says in 1 Corinthians 7:5. '*Defraud ye not one the other, except it be with consent for a time, that ye may give yourselves to fasting and prayer; and come together again, that Satan tempt you not for your incontinency.*' In other words, you two need to come together so you're not tempted to look for somebody else to make you happy." Mary spoke with concerned intensity, hoping Rene would hear the deep feeling behind her words.

The shade bristled at Mary's wise advice. Would she succeed in undoing his hard work?

Rene swatted a hand at the air in dismissal. "Oh, Mama, nothing like that is going to happen. We are fine. It's just- "

"-been three weeks since you and your husband have been together?" Mary interrupted.

"Mama, what did you need?" Rene had no patience for her mother's counsel this morning. Wrath was cheered by her abrupt response.

Arthur stirred on the couch. He started to wake up and noticed his mother-in-law in the room.

"Hi, Mama Mary. It's good to see you." He tried to gather the pillow and blanket to one side without being too obvious, but he noticed her sharp look. "Uhm, uh, I, uh, I fell asleep on the couch watching this good movie and…" He faltered under her gaze.

"Um-hum, that's what your wife says, too. I didn't know they had made *that* many good movies."

"You know, you always seem to stop by when I fall asleep on the couch. Why don't you c'mon and sit down, Mama Mary?" He gestured toward the couch.

"No, baby, I can't stay. I just came by to see if Rene wanted to go to this Women's conference with me next week, but I think she should- "

"...go, so I can get some Word in me and pray these *wicked spirits* out of my house?" Rene stared straight at Arthur as she interrupted her mother.

"No! I was going to say I think you two should let me keep the kids this weekend and take a trip somewhere." Mary's response came out sharper than she intended, but Rene's rudeness had surprised her.

Arthur shook his head. "Naw, that's okay. Thanks for offering but I think my *wife* would much rather enjoy spending time with a lot of women at a conference than spending time with her husband!" Rene clucked her tongue in derision. "And besides, we planned a trip three weeks ago and it fell through."

"Yes, Mama, he already took a trip by himself three weeks ago to Florida and didn't want me to go." Rene nearly spat the words in her contempt.

"Didn't want you to go! Don't you lie in front of your mama. We were supposed to go together and you..." Arthur sputtered. "You know what, I'm not going to do this, not in front of your mother." He grabbed up the pillow and blanket and started to walk away.

"Arthur, sweetheart, wait a minute," Mary pleaded. Arthur kept walking.

Rene folded her arms. "Mama, just let him go. He always running away like a *big baby!*" She yelled the last two words in Arthur's direction.

"Rene, you can't keep going on like this. This is not healthy for you or your children." She grabbed Rene by both shoulders. "Baby, your children can see what's going on and that's not good. Rene, somebody has to let go of their pride and follow the word of God. Both of you know the Word, but neither of you are living by the Word."

"But, Mama, you don't know how he treats …"

"I don't want to hear it. You've got to fix this! Be that Woman of God you are always speaking and teaching about. Don't look at what Arthur is doing; baby, you gotta look at yourself!"

Mary gave Rene a final hug before she left. As she walked out of the house, she said a silent prayer for her family members there and interceded with God on their behalf.

Rene pace the living room for a few minutes, thinking about what her mother said. She didn't like the situation any more than her mother did. She made her decision and headed toward the bedroom to try to mend things with Arthur. Wrath stepped out into the middle of the room and got between her and the hall.

Rene stopped, compelled by a force she couldn't name. The shadowy figure stepped closer and whispered in her ear.

"Girl, that stuff yo mama said might work for old folks, not for a woman like you. You got this! You're successful, you're smart and everybody likes you. But **him**? What you need him for? He don't do nothing but give you headaches. Don't say anything to him. Just keep doing what you're doing, and he'll see what he's been missing." Wrath chuckled at his own cleverness.

As the ideas filled Rene's mind, she questioned her mother's wisdom. "Why, she's not having to deal with what I deal with. Who is she to tell me how to act towards my own husband?" She began singing to herself. "He's gonna miss me..." and picked up her purse. There was a new store in town she wanted to check out and this was as good a time as any.

Wrath laughed aloud at the results of his handiwork as he watched her leave.

Chapter Six

"Lie not one to another, seeing that ye have put off the old man with his deeds; And have put on the new man, which is renewed in knowledge after the image of him that created him."
Colossians 3:9-10

Arthur pushed open the back door and held it for his brother. Both were hot and sweaty from a friendly, but hard-fought pickup game of basketball.

"Hey, Greg, you want some water?" Arthur offered as he headed to the refrigerator.

"Yeah, man. Whew, it is some hot out there." He took the chilled bottle from Arthur and rolled it across his forehead before he opened it. "Where's Rene and the kids? I thought they would have been here. I wanted to get her to make me a cheesecake. You know my sister-in-law makes the best cheesecakes!" He tipped his head back to take a big swig from the bottle.

"I don't know where they are, and I'm sure she would be glad to make YOU a cheesecake." He opened his own water and drank deeply.

Gregory nearly choked at his brother's words. "What do you mean by that?"

35

"By what? I just said she would be glad to make you a cheesecake. I don't know what you're talking about."

"Uh, uh, brother, you don't get out of it that easy. You put emphasis on the word YOU like you get some kind of problem with her making me a cheesecake. If so, bro, just say so. Don't be so sly about it."

"Look, Greg, I don't have a problem with Rene making cheesecakes for you and nobody else. But I do have a problem with her doing things for everybody else and making me second in her life. Man, that stuff gets old!" Arthur felt a sense of relief at describing the situation out loud after holding it in so long.

"Wait a minute, man. It sounds like you two are having some problems. Is it that bad?" Gregory couldn't believe his brother's marriage might be in trouble.

Wrath listened from the hall, pleased to hear Arthur admit the problems. It would be much harder to backtrack now the words had been spoken aloud.

Arthur's shoulders sank as he answered. "Man, I've been sleeping on the couch for a month! We go to church, talk to everybody, laugh, sing, praise God like everything's fine. Then we come home and act like total strangers. She goes to the bedroom. I go to the couch. Look, it's gotten so bad 'til I don't want to eat her food no more." He paused at the look of surprise on Gregory's face. "Yeah, I won't eat nothing she cook, whenever she decides to cook, that is. Because she's always gone helping somebody, or gone with the kids, or at the church, but she's never here when I need her."

"Arthur, have you two talked to Pastor Wilson about this? It seems like y'all need some counseling, man."

"Counseling!? Are you crazy? Don't nobody need no kind of counseling! And I don't need to talk to Pastor Wilson about this. If I have him all in my business, then that will be his sermon Sunday. I don't need his help."

Wrath cheered Arthur's statement. The last thing he wanted was for the family to get Christian counseling.

Gregory put his hand on Arthur's shoulder. "C'mon, man. Why is it so hard for you to sit down with your wife and your Pastor and the two of you talk this out? Don't you know the enemy wants to keep you two right where you are? Not talking, not sleeping together, just going through the mechanics of marriage. Man, that's not healthy! You know what the Word says in Ephesian 5:25 – 'Husbands, love your wives, even as Christ also loved the church, and gave himself for it.' What have you given to your wife?"

Arthur brushed his brother's hand away and started to walk away.

"Do you really love her as Christ loves the church and gave himself for it?" As Gregory continued to try to reach his brother, Wrath stepped in and caused him to choke. The demon couldn't have such talk touching Arthur's heart.

Arthur started to pound his brother on the back to help. "Man, you just don't know. You don't know how she is. You only see her at church, but you don't know what it's like living with her. I mean she does EVERYTHING for EVERYBODY and then she's too tired to spend time with me. Like I said, she's gone with the kids, she's – "

Gregory took a deep breath and interrupted his brother. "I heard you earlier! Man, you don't get it. Do you know why your wife is always doing things and helping people? It's because those other people can see her worth, and you don't. You've got a good woman living right here with you and you can't see it." He paused for another breath.

"She's beautiful, loves the Lord, a wonderful mother, and most of all, she loves your rusted behind! Don't you remember when the two of you were dating? Those were the very things you used to talk to me about. Always saying '*Man, she is so smart; man, she is so kind. She's always helping at the church and helping me with stuff. Man, that's somebody I could see me married to. She's going to be my wife one day.*' Well, guess what! You got her, and been having her for the last seventeen years, and still don't know how to treat her!"

Fury filled Wrath's face at Gregory's words. How dare this human try to interfere!? He concentrated his control on Arthur's response.

"Man, all you are saying is nice, but you ain't married. Oh, wait, you don't even have a woman! How do you think you can come in here telling me how to treat my wife, when you couldn't keep a wife for six months! Man, please. Get a woman first and keep her, then come and talk to me."

"Yeah, you're right, bro," Gregory answered. "But I can tell you I know I was full of pride. I allowed wrath to come in the middle of my marriage. If I had it to do all over again, I would have kicked pride and wrath out, and would love my woman better than I love myself!" He shook his head and turned toward the door. With a last look over his shoulder, he spoke once more. "I'm gone, bro, but I can tell you, you don't know what you have until it's gone. You need to talk to your wife, man, and always keep the lines of communication open. If the devil can stop you from talking to one another, his job is done. See ya later."

"Yeah, alright, man. I'll holler at you later." Thoughts swirled through Arthur's head as he watched his brother go. Could Greg be right? Maybe he was acting out of pride.

Wrath stepped close to Arthur's ear and whispered in his polished tone. "Man, how can he tell you something? He don't even have nobody! And what is he talking about, going to the Pastor? What can the Pastor tell you that you don't already know? I mean, you are a Minister and you know the Word for yourself. He telling you love your wife as Christ loved the church. How can you when she supposed to be submissive? Hah! Man, you got to keep sleeping on the couch and show her who's running things around here." He laughed softly to himself as he walked away from the bemused man.

Arthur headed into the bedroom and opened his closet. He picked through the clothes hanging there, anxious to select the perfect outfit to wear to church. As he checked out the contents, he started to sing to himself, "I'm the man." He would look good!

Chapter Seven

"Now the parable is this: The seed is the word of God. Those by the way side are they that hear; then cometh the devil, and taketh away the word out of their hearts, lest they should believe and be saved. They on the rock are they, which, when they hear, receive the word with joy; and these have no root, which for a while believe, and in time of temptation fall away. And that which fell among thorns are they, which, when they have heard, go forth, and are choked with cares and riches and pleasures of this life, and bring no fruit to perfection. But that on the good ground are they, which in an honest and good heart, having heard the word, keep it, and bring forth fruit with patience." Luke 8:11-15

Rene walked with her mother and Helen up the church walkway on Sunday morning. Malcolm and Marie followed just behind them. They could hear the music building as they neared the familiar sanctuary. Rene felt a peace enter her as they stepped through the doors. She loved the music, the message, the sense of coming home. The turmoil filling her marriage seemed to drain away while she was in worship.

Strange as it felt to walk in without Arthur at her side, she wouldn't stop her church attendance on his account. Let him answer the questions about why they didn't arrive together. She had the rest of her family around her.

She greeted friends as they made their way to their normal seats. Their group nearly filled the pew. The empty seat at the end caused her a momentary pang of grief, but she pushed it aside. Arthur made his own decisions and didn't consult her these days. So be it!

Once the service started, she made a concentrated effort to focus on Pastor Wilson's message. She could always count on spiritual nourishment through his words.

"Let the church say Amen," he called from the pulpit.

The congregation said, "Amen."

"Let the church say AMEN!" he boomed.

"AMEN!" came the response, filling the sanctuary with emotion.

"John 3:16 says: For God so loved the world that he gave His only begotten Son, that whosoever believeth in him should not perish, but have everlasting life." The pastor's conviction colored his words.

Arthur walked into the church as Pastor Wilson continued.

"Since God so loved the world, why is it so hard for us to love one another? Tell me, how can we jump, shout, sing and dance, but we can't speak to the person sitting next to us? Or better yet, we can't even speak to the people in our own house!"

The congregation reacted with a drawn out "Ohhhh."

"But we say we love the Lord. Don't you know we are lying? How we say, 'I love you, Lord' and husbands and wives sleeping in separate rooms, not speaking for weeks? I'm not talking about the world out there that God gave His only Son for. I'm talking about those that say they believe!"

Another wave of consternation swept through the gathered people.

"Church, we've got to stop lying and get real with ourselves, because we are not fooling God! We've got to stop playing church and allow this word to live in us and truly work in us. Amen!"

The church responded with a solemn "Amen."

The minister of music stood to lead the next hymn, but Rene barely heard the lyrics. Pastor Wilson's words seemed aimed right at her this morning. Her mind raced with mixed emotions.

When the service concluded, Rene paused to answer a question from her mother. Over Mary's shoulder, she could see Sister Kelly hurry over to Arthur. She glanced around for help from her children or brother-in-law, but Gregory and Pastor Wilson were talking near the front of the church while Malcolm and Marie were on the other side of the room chatting with friends. Malcolm seemed determined to get close to one of Marie's girlfriends by teasing his sister.

Rene resigned herself to finishing the conversation with her mother, even as she watched Sis Kelly move ever closer to Arthur.

Arthur took a step back from Sis Kelly's approach. She seemed to be in a big hurry to get closer to him than he was comfortable with.

"Hi, Minister Miller! You sure are looking nice today." Her voice seemed a little syrupy to him.

"Hey, Sis Kelly." He gave her a 'church family' hug, then pushed her to arm's length. "Thanks, you're looking mighty nice yourself. And that hat, that hat is bad, but in a good way." It couldn't hurt anything to return her compliment, could it?

The woman responded with an even bigger smile. "Why, thank you, Minister." She patted the edge of her hat. "You know, I cooked some chicken today, and you are more than welcome to come by for dinner. There's plenty." She looked up at him through thick eyelashes.

"Oh, thank you, Sis Kelly, but I think Rene cooked. I did enjoy the plate you gave me last week, though. That food was off the chain!"

"You really enjoyed it? I'm so glad. Did you get my text this morning?"

"Yes, yes, I did," Arthur nodded as he spoke.

"You know, I always like sending those inspirational words to everybody. I hope they help you throughout your day."

Arthur recognized her approach as flattery, but he enjoyed it just the same. "Uh, well, you know, they do help me, and I really enjoy them. It's good to know you're thinking about me at 6:00 in the morning. That's more than I can say some people do."

The two of them laughed together.

"Now, minister, I'm sure your wife gets up with you and spends time with you early in the morning. I mean, I would do that for my man. I would rub his tired shoulders at night, massage his feet, cook him --"

Gregory walked up and interrupted the conversation. "Hey, Bro, we're getting ready to leave. Are you coming?"

Arthur stuttered as he answered his brother. "Oh, yeah, yeah, I'm coming. Uh, Sis Kelly, it was good talking with you. Keep texting me and thanks for the invitation."

"Okay, bye and enjoy your day, minister. I'll Facebook you schedule lunch this week."

"Okay, do that." Arthur saw the disapproval on his brother's face.

He watched as Sis Kelly threw a smirk at Rene across the empty pews. Oh, man, how did this whole mess look to his wife?

"Rene, Rene, are you listening to me?" Mary tapped her daughter's arm.

"Sorry, Mama, I guess I was daydreaming for a minute," Rene answered as she fought the anger rising in her. How dare Sis Kelly try to make a move on Arthur! And him a married man, even if he wasn't acting like it at the moment.

"I asked if you had plans for dinner. I put a roast in the slow cooker before I got ready for church this morning. We could have a regular family dinner, if you want. We can invite Greg to join us."

"That sounds nice, Mama, but it looks like Arthur may have other plans."

"You don't know if you don't ask. I'll just give the two of them my invitation and see what they say. It would mean a lot to me to see all of you gathered around the table together." Mary patted her daughter on the shoulder, then headed over to Arthur and Gregory.

"C'mon, kids, let's go," Rene called to her children. She headed out the door to wait on the front steps of the church. Pastor Wilson approached her as she waited for them to join her.

'Hey, Rene, how are you today?"

"Hey, Pastor, I'm well, thanks."

"Are you sure?" He gave her a look up and down. "You look a little under the weather. You're not sick, are you?"

Rene shook her head and smiled, grateful for his consideration.

"Tell that husband of yours to take you home and nurse you back to health." The two of them laughed. "I was just the other day telling Minister Miller how the two of you are a great example of a wonderful family. I look at the two of you and your beautiful children, and I say, 'Lord, that is one fine family.'"

Rene tried to smile, even as tears filled her eyes. She cleared her throat before she answered him.

"Well, um, thank you for those wonderful words, Pastor. Um, I enjoyed the sermon today. Your message really hit home."

"Rene, that is what God wants it to do. Hit home, so homes can be changed. I'll see you later. I think my wife is beckoning me. She's ready to go and eat. I'd best lock up and get on. Take care."

"Thanks, Pastor. You do the same."

"Bye, Ms. Mary, Sis Bradford," he called as he waved farewell to the two ladies as they headed toward Rene.

The two of them responded in kind.

"So, baby, what was that all about?" asked Mary.

"Nothing, I was just telling him how good the sermon was. I hope Arthur was listening, because that word was just for him!" Rene answered.

"Alright, now. Remember what I told you. Look at yourself first before you start looking at somebody else," Mary chided.

Helen chimed in with enthusiasm. "Yeah, that's right, girl, 'cuz you see, I was looking at myself in the mirror this morning, and I said 'Helen, you surely do need to get your hair done. Why you was talking about J'naiqua's hair at work the other day?' And you need to get your nails done and..."

"Helen, baby, I think you may be standing too close to the formaldehyde at work," Mary interrupted. "How can you be so smart and act so dumb? I just don't understand it. But anyway, Rene, this has been going on for almost two months. Did you cook that handsome man of yours some dinner? Because my little old roast can wait."

"Yes, mother, I did. But as he probably told you, he'd rather go out to eat with his brother and some friends. He didn't ask me if I wanted to go. So, are you all coming by for dinner? I made a BIG meal and some cheesecakes."

"Oh, girl!" Helen exclaimed. "Yes, I'm coming by! You know I love your cheesecakes! Oh!! Count me in."

Malcolm and Marie joined them and the five of them left the churchyard to head for dinner at Rene's home.

Arthur watched them leave as he and Gregory made plans to meet friends for a game of basketball. He wondered if Rene had made her usual Sunday dessert of cheesecake with berries and whipped cream topping. Nothing he could order at a restaurant tasted nearly as good as Rene's cheesecake, but he sure wasn't willing to back down and let her win just to get some cheesecake. No way!

Bishop Billie Jackson

Chapter Eight

"Wherefore let him that thinketh he standeth take heed lest he fall. There hath no temptation taken you but such as is common to man: but God is faithful, who will not suffer you to be tempted above that ye are able; but will with the temptation also make a way to escape, that ye may be able to bear it." I Corinthians 10:12-13

A few days later, Arthur and Sis Kelly walked out of the casual dining restaurant on the town square together. Each had an ice cream cone in hand. Sis Kelly giggled as Arthur raced to catch a melting line of ice cream before it fell from the cone.

"I'm so glad you were able to meet me for lunch today. This was so refreshing!" Sis Kelly paused. "It's a nice day out, I'm with a wonderful gentleman. I mean, what woman wouldn't be happy right now?" She batted her eyes at him as she licked her ice cream.

"Tell that to my wife," Arthur said. "It's hard for her to stop and do things like this. She's always running and going and..."

Sis Kelly interrupted him. "Well, that's enough about her. What about you? I know *some* things you like but tell me more." In her

mind, she was singing "*If I were your woman.*"
She wanted to learn everything she could about
Arthur so she could hone her approach.

As Arthur began to respond to her question,
his phone rang. He pulled it from his pocket and
checked the caller.

"Something important, minister?" asked Sis
Kelly.

"It's Rene. I'll call her back later. Well, I've
got to go. This was really nice, really nice."

"Yes, it was, Minister Miller. We should do
this and *more* again."

Before Arthur could respond, Pastor Wilson
and his wife walked up. They appeared shocked
to see the two church members together.
Everyone started talking at the same time in an
attempt to hide their discomfort.

"Well, hey there, Minister Miller, Sis Kelly.
It's good to see you two. Um, Minister, how is
Sis Rene these days?"

"Oh, she's, um, she's doing fine, Pastor."
Arthur spoke faster than normal. "In fact, she
just called me, and I'm headed home." He
laughed in an attempt to appear innocent. *After
all*, he told himself, *it was just lunch and ice
cream.*

"Well, that's fine. I would like to come by
and talk to you and Sis Rene about starting
couples' classes at the church. Like I've told
you both, you have a *wonderful* marriage and a

beautiful family." Pastor Wilson stared at Sis Kelly as though daring her to dispute his words.

"Okay, sure, I'll talk to Rene to see what's a good time for her and I'll give you a call." Arthur couldn't think of any other way to respond. Leading a class with Rene was a long way from what he was feeling these days.

"That's wonderful, *Minister*. I'll wait to hear from you." He emphasized Arthur's title, a subtle reminder to his coworker.

After goodbyes all around, they went their separate ways. Arthur hailed a taxi for Sis Kelly, before heading to his own car. He felt sure Pastor and Mrs. Wilson were judging him as they walked away.

"What would you think if you knew how bad my wife was treating me?" he wondered. *"Bet you wouldn't be so quick to think poorly of me if you realized what I had to put up with at home."*

He made his way back to his office, unaware of Wrath's delight in his rationalizations.

Bishop Billie Jackson

Chapter Nine

"Blessed is the man that endureth temptation: for when he is tried, he shall receive the crown of life, which the Lord hath promised to them that love him. Let no man say when he is tempted, I am tempted of God: for God cannot be tempted with evil, neither tempteth he any man: But every man is tempted, when he is drawn away of his own lust, and enticed. Then when lust hath conceived, it bringeth forth sin: and sin, when it is finished, bringeth forth death. Do not err, my beloved brethren." James 1:12-16

Arthur went home, confused and frustrated. He wasn't doing anything wrong, was he? Then why did he feel like he was in trouble? Just because he ran into Pastor Wilson and his wife didn't make an innocent lunch into something sinful!

Wrath waited just inside the door and glided to Arthur's side.

"Now all you did today was eat lunch with one of the saints of the church. So what if you know Sis Kelly is lusting after you? *You* haven't done *anything* wrong. If Rene asks you where you've been, all you need to say is 'I've been out.' She ain't yo mama and you don't have to answer to her for nothing. Remember, you the man!!" He whispered his poison into Arthur's ear.

"That's right," Arthur mumbled under his breath.

Rene came in from the kitchen. "Good evening."

"Evening," Arthur grunted back at her.

"So how was your day today?"

"Oh, my day was *GREAT!*" he answered, pouring every bit of sarcasm he could muster into his statement.

Rene chose to ignore his tone. "That's good. Are you ready to eat?"

"No. I ate something already and I'm not hungry."

Wrath moved over to Rene.

"He's been out with somebody else. He ain't been eating your food in months! Now where has he been eating? Huh??" His words cut to Rene's heart.

"I've noticed you haven't been eating here for almost two months. Where have you been eating and who have you been eating with? I've heard you on the phone, making your plans. I saw your Facebook posts!"

Wrath smiled as he returned to Arthur's side. "What is she talking about? Ain't nothing wrong with you talking to women on the phone or on Facebook. You need to delete her as your friend! And nothing is wrong if you are hungry and they are hungry, and you decide to go out and eat with them or even eat the food they cook for you. You are the head of this house, and she's the one that's supposed to submit, not you!"

"Woman, don't come at me like that! I eat where I want to eat and with whomever I want to eat with," Arthur fired at Rene. "And you are too nosey! I ought to delete you as my Facebook friend! I'm the head of this house – me, I'm the man! I don't need you coming at me with all these questions. I think we need to either separate or just go ahead and get a divorce. I can't keep living like this!"

Wrath started laughing so hard he had to sit down in the middle of the floor. It was working! His plan was working to perfection!

Arthur paused to take a breath then continued. "I need somebody who will spend time with me, love me in action and not just in words. I need someone I can trust to have MY back in everything I do!" He shouted the last sentence.

Rene was thrown a step back by his anger. How dare he!?!

"What? Are you serious? After two kids and seventeen years of marriage, you waltz in here and say you want a divorce! You never cease to amaze me. You walk around here and all you can think about is what I haven't' done for you! Well, what have you done for me? Huh? Nothing but fuss and complain, fuss and complain!"

Wrath rolled on the floor in glee. This just got better and better!

"Are you ever happy?" Rene asked Arthur. "Do you ever really want to be here with me and the kids? You don't act like it, because you are always fussing when I ask you to help me with them. You deal with your children only when you feel like dealing with them, and that is very rare. You say you can't trust ME. What about Sis Kelly bringing plates of food for only YOU to eat and telling you she cooked chicken for YOU to come by and eat. What kind of mess is that when you have a wife and kids at home? I don't ever remember her asking *me* over for dinner or bringing *ME* and our kids some food! That's crazy. Guess what, *I can't trust You*! My husband hasn't slept in the bed with me for over two months! You don't eat my food. You hug and talk to everybody else at church and barely look at me."

Malcolm and Marie came out of their rooms to see what the commotion was. As they came under the influence of Wrath's presence, they began to argue with each other. Rene tried to separate them and calm them but didn't succeed. Malcolm slammed out the front door. Marie ran back to her bedroom in tears. Rene could only stand in confusion as her family went to pieces around her. Arthur shook his head in disgust as he spread the pillow and blanket on the couch. When he prepared to lay down, Rene rolled her eyes and retreated to her own bedroom.

Wrath pumped his skeletal arm in victory.

Bishop Billie Jackson

Chapter Ten

"Now we beseech you, brethren,
by the coming of our Lord Jesus
Christ, and by our gathering
together unto him, That ye be not
soon shaken in mind, or be
troubled, neither by spirit, nor by
word, nor by letter as from us, as
that the day of Christ is at hand.
Let no man deceive you by any
means: for that day shall not
come, except there come a falling
away first, and that man of sin be
revealed, the son of perdition." II
Thessalonians 2:1-3

Arthur answered the door to find Pastor
Wilson with his finger on the doorbell, about to
push it again.

"Hi, Pastor Wilson. How are you? C'mon
in."

Wrath withdrew to a corner of the room to
watch what the man of God would do. Perhaps
he could lure him into discordance along with
the Millers. What a triumph that would be!

"Thank you, Minister Miller," the pastor
replied. "I'm doing well. How about you?"

"I'm doing good. Yeah, things are going
well." He motioned Pastor Wilson toward the
couch. "Have a seat."

Malcolm and Marie came into the living room.

"Hey, Pastor Wilson! Didn't expect to see you." Malcolm reached out to shake hands with his pastor.

"Hi, kids. How are things going for you?"

"We're doing fine," Marie answered.

"Yeah, fine," Malcolm echoed. "Dad, where's Mom?"

"She's in her room," Arthur answered. "Go tell her Pastor Wilson is here."

"I'll tell her, dad," Marie offered. She walked to the other side of the couch and yelled down the hallway. "Mom! Dad said Pastor Wilson is here!"

"Thanks, baby, but I could have done that myself," Arthur commented.

Marie looked embarrassed and headed back to her room. Malcolm headed into the kitchen.

Rene entered the living room and greeted Pastor Wilson with warmth. "Hi, Pastor. How nice to see you! How are you?"

"Hey, Sis Rene. I'm well. How are you?" he replied. "You're looking good as always."

Rene smiled at his compliment. "Thank you. What is this special visit for?"

Pastor Wilson stuttered in confusion. "Well, uh, I uh…"

Arthur interrupted. "Sorry, Pastor, I forgot to tell Rene you wanted us to start a couples' class at the church."

"Us!?!" Rene exploded in surprise. "Pastor, are you sure you want *us* to start couples' classes at the church? I just don't know."

"And why wouldn't I?" he asked. "You all have a beautiful family and a wonderful marriage."

Wrath eased his way closer, anxious to catch every word.

"Oh, Pastor, if only you knew..." Rene said. She shook her head in sadness and looked away.

"Is there something you're trying to say, Sis Rene?"

"No, no, forget I said it. Would you like something to drink? I made a fresh pitcher of iced tea just an hour ago."

"No, Rene, thank you for asking but I think you need to sit and be still for a moment." The pastor's expression carried his concern for a member of his flock who was plainly in distress.

"Yeah, you right about that," Arthur interjected, as he shook his head.

"Uh, brother, do you have something you'd like to share?" Pastor Wilson asked Arthur.

"Oh, no, I'm fine, we are all fine. There's nothing wrong here." Arthur said, and plopped on the end of the couch. Wrath smiled at his denial.

"You know, what makes a wonderful family and marriage is not everything going our way. It's communicating with each other, talking about your problems without anger and strife and not allowing *Wrath to come in the middle*. Neither one of you have come to talk to me, but for the last two months, I've noticed distance between the two of you. I've noticed times before when you two were upset with one another, but this, this is different. It's like that spark I used to see in your eyes is no longer there. What happened?"

Arthur and Rene started to speak at the same time, talking over each other in an effort to give their side of the story and explain why they were in the right.

"One at a time, please. I can't understand what you're saying when you're both talking at once," Pastor Wilson pleaded.

"Pastor, first off, we are fine," Arthur insisted. "But since you asked, you just don't know my wife. You see her at church, but..." he hesitated. "The fact is, I don't trust her. She puts everything and everybody in front of me. There's always something or somebody else that's more important. I don't mind her helping at the church, but my goodness, she puts me on the back burner for everything. We don't ever have any time to spend together. It's like she has her life and I have mine."

Wrath wriggled in discomfort. If Arthur and Rene told this pastor what was happening, he might lose the ground he had gained with them. He focused on Rene and concentrated his attention on influencing her response.

"Do you *hear* him?" Rene said. "It's always what I don't do for him. He walks around here mad at the world. He'll be mad just because it's a new day!" she sneered.

"He fusses about everything. He don't want to spend time with me or the children. He sleeps on the couch. He won't eat my food, and now he says he wants a divorce! He don't think I know he talks to Sis Kelly on the phone at all hours and she cooks for him. He won't even eat MY food, but he eats hers."

Rene started crying. "She's not even his wife. Pastor, I'm sorry, but I think you have the wrong couple. I really don't think you want *us* to head a couples' class when we can't even keep our own family together." She collapsed on the opposite end of the couch and buried her face in her hands.

Pastor Wilson stopped and said a silent prayer before he responded. He could feel the presence of Wrath in the room and knew his words could allow this this couple to slip further into the chaos or lead them out of it and back into harmony. He sank into the arm chair opposite the couch.

"I want you two to move closer to each other."

Rene and Arthur looked at him in horror. Closer? They had never felt more distant from each other.

"I mean it. Move closer and join hands. I'm speaking as your pastor now, your spiritual leader."

The couple inched toward the center of the couch until they were close enough to join hands. Wrath cringed as they touched.

"Good. Now, Wrath has been all up in your house, trying to destroy your marriage. Do you know who Wrath is? The Bible says in Ephesians 4:26 and 27, 'Be ye angry, and sin not: let not the sun go down upon your wrath: Neither give place to the devil.' Wrath is a person who goes to bed with saved people when we don't forgive before we lay down to sleep. When we hear Wrath talking to us, we listen and react to the suggestions he gives."

He looked at the couple. Both of them sat with heads bowed, listening to his words. He could feel the struggle in the room as Wrath fought to maintain his control of the Millers.

"Now, Arthur, you know the Word of God! You know Ephesians 5 speaks of a husband loving his wife as he loves his own body. My question to you, brother is, *do you love yourself?* If so, you wouldn't walk around so angry and fussing all the time, but rather find it a joy and a pleasure to spend time with your own wife and kids. You wouldn't look for somebody else to make you feel good. Loving yourself isn't just making sure your clothes look good or your hair is cut right. Brother, I mean do you *love who you are within*, because if you don't, it will be hard for you to love *anyone without!*"

He turned his attention to Rene. "Rene, in that same book, it tells the wives to submit to Your Own husband; but sister, you are submitting to everyone else but him. It's good to do 'good' things, but that is a *sacrifice!* Because it is better to be *obedient!* And my dear, you are not being obedient, when you don't make time for your husband. Say no sometimes, even to me! THIS is your head," he said, pointing to Arthur. "He is your husband!"

Wrath tried to overcome the message of Pastor Wilson's words, but Arthur and Rene were deep in prayer and contemplation of what they had heard. Frustration grew in the shadow's demeanor as he watched his work being undercut by the Word of God.

Pastor Wilson resumed his lesson.

"Wives walk around wondering why their husbands get on these chat sites or seek attention from another woman. It's because wives are not making themselves available to spend time with their husbands. Yes, you have the kids, job, church and so many other things, but don't forget about your partner, that man who you used to look up to and love so much.

Daughter, I'm not saying it's right for men to act that way, or for your husband to act the way he does. But you have *got* to show your husband he is the most important person to you. And Arthur, you've got to be willing to help her with the kids and be supportive and patient."

Pastor Wilson rose from the arm chair. Wrath trembled in fear of what the pastor would say next.

"Now, you two need to kick Wrath out and keep Wrath out of your home."

Rene and Arthur looked at each other. They spoke together, "Get out, Wrath." Wrath breathed a little easier at the weakness of their command. He could stand easily against such soft resistance.

"No, no," said Pastor Wilson, urging them to greater commitment. "You need to **kick Wrath out** and tell him to **FLEE**! You've got to mean it! When you resist the devil, he will flee! Resist that temptation, resist that anger, resist frustration! **Resist Wrath and tell him to flee from your marriage and your children in the Name of Jesus**!"

The three of them joined together in ordering Wrath to flee. Wrath backed away from their united words but didn't leave the property entirely. He hid in the bushes outside the door. Maybe he could win this battle yet.

Arthur and Rene embraced, then folded Pastor Wilson into the hug. He offered a blessing on their behalf before leaving.

Wrath slipped back in the door before they closed it. He took refuge in the corner of the living room.

An hour later, Sis Kelly walked up to the front door of the Miller home and rang the bell. Arthur answered the door.

"Sis Kelly, what are you doing here?" he asked, surprised by her brazen appearance at his home.

"Hi, Minister, Miller. How are you today?" She smiled and gazed up through her eyelashes.

"I'm fine, thank you. I repeat, what are you doing here?"

"Why, I wanted to know if you would like to have lunch tomorrow."

Wrath listened for Arthur's response. Perhaps his cause was not lost after all.

Arthur took a deep breath and stood tall. "No, sister, actually. I won't be having lunch with you anymore. Also, please don't cook anymore food for me unless you have enough for my wife and kids, too."

Sis Kelly gasped at the strength of his answer.

"I should never have led you on to think it was okay for us to talk like we do. That was my fault and I'm sorry. I should never have taken food from you or taken you to lunch. My brother is a wonderful single man, but I am a wonderfully happily married man. Oh, and if you need prayer in the future, call my wife and ask her to pray with you. Goodbye, sister."

She "hummphed" as he closed the door. Sis Kelly turned her back to the offending door and walked away mumbling to herself. "Well, I know his brother has money and he cute, too. So, Bro Gregory *may* be a better catch for me anyway."

Chapter Eleven

"My son, despise not the
chastening of the LORD; neither
be weary of his correction: For
whom the LORD loveth he
correcteth; even as a father the
son in whom he delighteth.
Happy is the man that findeth
wisdom, and the man that getteth
understanding. For the
merchandise of it is better than
the merchandise of silver, and the
gain thereof than fine gold."
Proverbs 3:11-14

When Rene went to bed that night, she
found Arthur already there. He faced the wall
and his back was turned to the center of the bed.
She shook her head, saddened that he seemed to
be asleep without them having a chance to talk.
She slid under the covers on her side and faced
her own wall. Wrath watched from the doorway.

"Father, I thank You for this second chance
with my marriage," she heard Arthur say, his
voice throbbing with emotion. "I will do all in
my power to honor You and the precious wife
You have given me."

Rene's heart raced. He wasn't asleep
without her, he was praying for her!

Arthur rose from the bed. "No, we will not
be back to back. Wrath, get out of here. I sent

you away once and I refuse to let you back in." He paced the room, going from one corner to the other and covering every open foot of the room. "I'm the head of this house, and I will resist the devil. Wrath, because I have resisted you, you must flee this house, never to return! In Jesus' Name!"

Wrath withdrew from the house in tears, defeated by the faith of the couple.

Arthur grabbed Rene in his arms as he felt the tension dissipate. "I love you honey. Please forgive me. I *will* love you as Christ loves the church from here on. We are in this together, forever."

"I love you, too, honey!" Rene said, as she looked into his eyes and delighted in the warmth she saw there. "And I am with you until the end."

Wrath slunk down the street, peering into every house he passed. He looked for the tiniest seed of dissension or indifference. When he found it, he would enter a new home, ready to wreck it and resume his destructive work.

The question is, will it be yours?

Meet Apostle B.R. Jackson

Apostle B. R. Jackson is the Founder/Senior Pastor of Rivers of Living Waters in Gulfport, Mississippi, and the founder of The Vision of The Elohim Ministry.

He has been married to Prophetess Carolyn Jackson for 42 years. They were childhood sweethearts, first meeting 47 years ago. In this union, God has blessed them with five daughters: Crystal, Christian, Candra ,Carmela and Charnele; and fourteen grandchildren: Ja'Marion, Ja'Liyah, Ja'Kaila, Ja'Siah , Jaira, Skylar, Chloe , Aiden, Ny'King, Cornell, Cornelius, Emperor, Kashton and as of this writing, baby Rhyker is on the way. He also has another granddaughter, Destiny, which means "before Christ."

Apostle Jackson began ministering on 4 March 1984 under the leadership of Pastor Freddie Owens. He moved forward in his spiritual learning under the guidance of Overseer Charles Taylor and Bishop O.G. Rankin.

While Apostle Jackson serves as Senior Pastor of a local church, he is also called of God to serve other Pastors and church leaders. He is appointed by God to impact the lives of many across the country. Apostle Jackson was consecrated a Bishop in November 1993. He was consecrated and set aside as an Apostle in

July of 2002. Apostle Jackson became an ordained Bishop with the Church of God in November 2004. On March 20, 2008, Apostle Jackson finished his studies and graduated from The School of Prophets in North Carolina. Apostle Jackson has also completed some courses with Slidell Baptist Seminary.

He is a born-again saint filled with the Holy Spirit. With the help of the Lord he has set up and established a Jamaican church in Mississippi and built one church in Kenya, Africa. He has also received an Honorary Doctrine of Divinity from Cambridge University. Born and raised in Gulfport, Mississippi, he served in the US Army and is a Vietnam Veteran.

He has done over ten years of street preaching and at the present time he oversees eleven churches.

Wrath in the Middle marks his first book.